SERIES INTRODUCTION

The Grattan Street Shorts series is designed to showcase outstanding writing that does not fit neatly into conventional formats. It includes novellas, linked short stories, collected microfiction, long essays, fictocriticism and experimental memoir, and features the work of emerging writers particularly, but not exclusively. Each volume also includes a commentary by a leading scholar or writer in the field.

MER

SAMANTHA AMY MANSELL

 **Grattan Street Press**

ABOUT THE AUTHOR

Samantha is an editor and writer living in Sydney. She is passionate about intersectional feminism, bisexual representation in literature, and creating fantastical worlds. *Mer* is her first book.

Published by Grattan Street Press 2020

Grattan Street Press is the imprint of the
teaching press based in the School of Culture
and Communication at the University of
Melbourne, Parkville, Australia.

THE UNIVERSITY OF
MELBOURNE

Grattan Street Press
School of Culture and Communication
John Medley Building,
Parkville, VIC 3010
www.grattanstreetpress.com

Cover by Michael Skinner © Grattan Street Press, 2020.
Typeset in Adobe Caslon Pro

Printed in Australia

ISBN: 9780648209645

A catalogue record for this book is available from the
National Library of Australia

For Lucy and Sunni,
I couldn't have survived without you

Contents

AUTHOR NOTE

To approach the Other in conversation is
to welcome his expression, in which at each
instant he overflows the idea a thought would
carry away from it. It is therefore to receive
from the Other beyond the capacity of the I,
which means exactly: to have the idea of infinity. But this also means: to be taught.

Emmanuel Levinas

The concept and first draft of *Mer* was originally conceived in a Contemporary Eco-Fiction course I took during my Master of Creative Writing, Publishing and Editing at the University of Melbourne. In one of the first tutorials of this course, in an exercise of questioning the anthropocene, our tutor took us outside and asked us to sit under a tree and imagine ourselves to be that tree. To imagine our spines extending beyond our skin, becoming roots in the earth.

I found a tree and I sat beneath it. Impossible, I thought. How could a conscious creature like myself ever imagine what it was like to be unconscious? How could I, with a body of nerves, conceive how a tree of wood and bark would experience sickness and pain? And what right did I have to even try? It was not possible that from within my own social and cultural framework, from within the bounds of the language and threshold of human experience, that I could ever define anything outside of myself.

It was this idea, the challenge of the Other, that I carried through the semester and which became 'The Deep'. Initially, it was the subversion of the fairytale I was most interested in. By mirroring Hans Christian Andersen's 'The Little Mermaid', I was playing with the predictable and familiar morality structure and questioning the patriarchal foundations of the fables fed to me as a young girl through books and Disney.

Inspired by Hélène Cixous ('If woman has always functioned "within" the discourse of man, a signifier that has always referred back to the opposite signifier which annihilates its specific energy and diminishes or stifles its very different sounds, it is time for her to dislocate this "within," to explode it, turn it around, and seize it; to make it hers, containing it, taking it in her own mouth, biting that tongue with her very own teeth to invent for herself a language to get inside of.') and Judith Butler ('The violence of language consists in its effort to capture the ineffable and, hence, to destroy it, to seize hold of that which must remain elusive for language to operate as a living thing'), I have always been fascinated by the power and action of language, and it was this that led me to explore the pronouns and identifiers surrounding the self-identification of the species of the mer – removing gendered language and bodies and replacing them with ones I created. This led to my creation of a binary based on species, rather than one of gender: per for the humans (which I have dubbed 'netters' in the merfolk's vernacular) and mer for the merfolk. When I was given the opportunity to expand 'The Deep' into this collection of stories, the motivation behind this became twofold as I carried the new language through. First, to continue in the tradition of science fiction in pushing the boundaries of gendered language, and, second, to create a purposeful discomfort, confusion and alienation for the reader (apologies). From the first line, I wanted you on the back foot, immediately Othered by the narrative. I hoped that by forcing you to adjust to a new form of language, I would leave you questioning the social construction of language and its impact on understanding and connection with characters and with literature itself.

However, as I cannot possibly have the 'idea of infinity', and the complete erasure and reinvention of language was not entirely possible, I personified the ocean as the bridge between the worlds of the netters and the merfolk. A conduit of possible understanding of the Other and also an attempt at gifting the environment agency.

Along with language in this dismantling of patriarchal structures, I played with the construction of bodies. The concept of the body often comes hand in hand with that of gender, and working with a mythological creature gave me a lot of room to move. Merfolk have long been depicted as highly sexualised women, designed to lure men into desire and death. Instead, I wanted to challenge this traditional idea of merfolk and sirens being designed for the male gaze and in the human image. In *Mer* I emphasise the merfolk's differences. I remove organs that would not make sense for them, such as ears, and create new ones such as their sensitive hair and the tendrils of their tails, which allow them to read vibrations in the water to understand 'sound' and distance. I also wanted merfolk to be more connected to and reflective of their environment, particularly as the environment could be considered a character in and of itself, and so the mer in each of the stories has a different physiology from the next. Ondine is large, serpentine, more human-size, as mer comes from the deep sea; Odel is small, a river fish, with eyes on either side of mer head rather than forward facing as Ondine's are; the reef mer are even smaller, the size of seahorses, and move in collective groups with hive minds; Unzel, the siren, actually designed to exist above the surface as a guardian of mer people, does have ears and lungs (as well as gills) in order to sing.

Furthermore, I wanted to play with the idea of transformation, with one body becoming another. In 'The Boat' we see a young netter transformed into a mer through the power of Unzel's song. Unzel too is a created species, crafted by the Merleader and the ocean as the perfect guardian of the ocean, a magic that tied mer to one place in order to survive. I was exploring the idea of how bodies can be prescriptive and restrictive for some, how we can be anchored by other people's expectations of us, and how family is often something that we make for ourselves rather than something biological.

Transformation of bodies was also an essential part of my highlighting of environmental destruction due to climate change. In each story I describe how the mers' bodies show signs of deterioration and damage, and portray the transformed seascape in which they exist with trash being a common feature in their environment, a 'disenchantment from the illusion of the green oasis ... totalising images of a world without refuge from toxic penetration' (Buell).

Exploring these ideas were challenges that my writing had to rise to meet, but I'm proud of the outcome. My next project will be something quite different as I move from a more literary style of fiction to my passion projects in YA fantasy. But I will still follow similar frameworks in challenging patriarchal structures and the reimagination of myths, legends and worlds.

Thank you for coming on this journey with me. I hope you'll be seeing my name in print someday again in the not too distant future.

WORKS CITED

Buell, Lawrence. *Writing for an Endangered World: Literature, Culture and Environment in the U.S. and Beyond.* Belknap Press, 2003.

Butler, Judith. *Excitable Speech: A Politics of the Performative.* Routledge, 1996.

Cixous, Hélène. 'The Laugh of the Medusa.' Translated by Keith Cohen and Paula Cohen. *Signs: Journal of Women in Culture and Society 1*, no. 4. (Summer, 1976): 875–893.

Levinas, Emmanuel. Translated by Lingis, Alphonso. *Totality and Infinity: A Essay on Exteriority.* Duquesne University Press, 1969.

Mer

THE REEF

We breathe with the current of the reef. We dance with the will of the water. Our tiny bodies spin to and fro with the tide and the trash. Sometimes we teeter on the edge of the drop-off only to dart with the stretch of our tails when a reef shark – or a net – ventures too close. We weave through the jellyfish, bounce across their tops and plunge with surprise when we discover that some aren't jellyfish at all, but clingy, suffocating imposters. Our hearts are the frantic beat of joy, even as we squirm from their grip.

The reef teems with life. And when the tide goes out, we're washed along the shallow corals. Epaulette sharks wriggle on spotted fins across the tiny protruding corals as they hunt for hidden crabs. When the ocean calls us back out, we sometimes try to grab onto their long tails, begging to stay with them in the low tide. But our heads spin without enough water for our gills, so we let go, rushing back into deeper reef waters, squirming with delight along the way.

The fish in the reef are often wary of us – they don't always like our games. The stingrays never forgive us for tugging on their barbs, though they would never sting us for it, and the black-tip reef sharks hate it when we ride on their dorsal fins. They remain silent – watchful. They know our sorrows. Sometimes we think that, maybe, it is not our games that they are wary of, but the curse that follows us. They have seen the rubble . . .

Our palace of vibrant orange sat on a deep shelf of the reef just metres from the seafloor. Our neighbours were schools of butterflies and angels, and we often saw turtles drifting by. But, one day, we returned to our palace in the dying light and our stomachs filled with an icy dread.

Five bristling shadows were latched to our coral home, gnawing at the staghorn. Three more devoured the coral upon the shelves. On the seafloor, no species – pillar, table, brain – was left untouched. We knew these monsters well – the crown-of-thorns starfish. Barely any of our palace

– our home – was visible between their dark mass and blood-red spikes. They were huge, ten times the size of our delicate, curled seahorse-like tails, their twenty arms still as rocks as they ate away reef after reef – trying to blend as if we would not notice their hideous bodies. Fear thrummed in our chests, heartbeats rattling like the ocean dragging the tide through rocks.

But we did not allow ourselves to be controlled by fear. With our small, sharp teeth bared, we swarmed them and yanked at their spines. Some snapped off in our hands, but not enough to compel them to break their grip. In our rage, we ignored the pain as they pricked and cut our soft underbellies.

We screeched, but we are no sirens, and our tails were not large enough to bat them away. The smallest of the merfolk, we have only our mischief to protect us from the whims of those who would do our miracle harm. On this day, though, mischief was not enough against the ravenous crown-of-thorns. One careened towards us, riding the current, its pale underbelly reaching to devour, maw wide. Luckily, we are as swift as we are small, and we darted out of the way, allowing it to latch in between two other crown-of-thorns. It settled in comfortably, consuming the last of the reef's colours.

We watched as our castle crumbled, and we were left adrift. Nomads on the current . . .

✖

As much as we love the thrill of spinning with the tide and exploring the expanse of the reef, with every flash of orange coral we feel the painful ache for home. More than a longing, we need the safety of the palace – with every rise of the sun over the surface, the warmth saps our energy.

Our gills work hard to breathe in the heat. We struggle to swim when our heads are spinning. We try to dart in and out of the tentacles of the anemones before they sting us, or keep up with the herd of our distant kin – the seahorses – dashing across the reef, so that we may try to find our frantic joy once more.

On the fourth moonrise of our homelessness, just as we think we can't go further, we see a shelf that almost looks like home. We dart towards it, eyes wide at the twisted columns that look like those of our palace. But, as we enter its arches, something feels wrong.

A slow, thick fear, like the black spill that once coated our reef, rises within us; the tendrils of our hair stand to attention. We reach out gently to listen. All we hear are the cries – a soft ripple through the water, a heart-breaking echo of the song our palace once sang.

The coral is scared. Trembling. Retreating.

Even as we watch, its tips lighten, almost colourless.

But there are no crown-of-thorns here, and so we curl together, tight and sad, and drift to sleep on the coral's sick croon.

We wake to a world of white. We are shaking as we emerge from our found sanctuary. Much of the coral and its song are almost lifeless, now paled and barely a tremble. Fear has won. This is a curse unlike anything we have known.

Our hearts crack like the thorns that we snapped in our hands.

Already, our neighbours have begun to flee and the waters have become empty and hollow like bowels of sunken ships claimed by the reefs.

We do not want to leave the reef, we cannot bear to lose another inch of our home. But the tide rushes out over our heads, and we let the current pull us further out to sea – to coral that has yet to give up. We huddle in crevices of a still-thriving part of the reef, stroking our tiny hands along its damaged surface and crooning along to its song. We hope for the darkness, the coolness, to come.

The coolness doesn't come, but the netters do.

In this part of the reef, where usually the only white is the flash of a fish's belly, they swarm without respite – eyes warped and protruding from their heads, the shells on their backs ensuring their weak lungs don't suffocate; their fake fins, an awkward, plastic imitation of our deep-sea kin, flapping behind. With each stroke and kick they narrowly miss the reef.

They seem harmless, admiring even. Sometimes we are tempted to reveal ourselves, just to see the wonder in their eyes. We are nothing more than a myth to them, and this is what protects us. So we stay in coral that is still vibrant, though its orange is only slightly paler than that of our palace. Here we try to build a home, but the tide carries with it our curse as the netters' joy breeds a careless abandon. Unable to cure the imbalances of the reef's population, the ocean and its all-seeing current are no match for the intrusion of the netters. They touch everything, feel everything, take pieces of us home to keep, or leave something behind for us to remember them. As if there isn't enough in our oceans for them to have left their mark.

A small pod swims together in the jerky, awkward way that netters do. The two smallest chase after a school of guppies, only to receive a warning gesture from their parents. The current undoes the smallest one's long hair – dead, unseeing hair – and it splays out around per in a poor mockery of our tendrils. The tie drifts through the water, catching on a column of our coral. The netterling turns, lands on the tie, then kicks down. A chubby finger loops inside and tugs. Our new home trembles with the force.

We dart forward and yank the netterling's long strands of hair. Per jerks, and bubbles explode from the contraption where per mouth should be. By the time per body writhes around to look for us, we are already hidden within the coral. There is nothing but the reef. Confused and frightened, the netterling kicks frantically to catch up to per family, tie abandoned. Satisfied, we bare our teeth, smile as sharp as the anger in our chests.

A shadow flickers in our periphery. Our hearts stop. The crown-of-thorns have found us again – we brought them here! We turn to fight – no, to flee – but . . . a netter appears instead, separated from the rest. Per stalks ungracefully behind a passing reef shark, per black, shiny body jittering with excitement.

Per unwieldy fins move with such a force through the water that an angelfish is spun off its path and soft corals bend away. The reef shark, not normally prey, has not noticed the netter.

A song of fear, of stress, swells from the shelves of coral around us. The song of the curse. Anger, fear, frustration – hot, cold, hot – flash through our bodies. And so, this time, we do not hide. This time we follow. The ocean's current urges us forward.

The netter chases the shark with a device pressed to per already modified eyes. Flashes spark. But the netter's lumbering jerks through the water are not enough to keep up with the elegant glide of the shark and, with another flash of light, per stops swimming and takes a moment to look around.

Bright yellow coral waves gently in the water, not yet touched by the crown-of-thorns plague, but a small patch next to a stunning purple polyp has paled. This curse chases us even here.

The netter dives down towards it, running rough hands over the dried and drained branches. Weak and skeletal, the brittle branch breaks in the netter's careless grip.

Perched behind a sponge, we hiss a stream of bubbles.

The netter brings the piece of coral close to per face, closing per fist around it and tucking it into a pocket at per waist. The netter barely even spares a glance around for witnesses to per theft. This time, the netter moves to the healthy coral, brushes the tip of per finger along the branch. We watch. Per finger stops at a small joint, then presses. Hard.

The snap reverberates through the water, setting every tiny scale on our bodies on edge. The snap is so loud it could have been one of our own bones. The netter moves to place this piece of coral in the pouch, with the other, when we surge forward on a wave of defiance.

Let the netter see us, let per toxic curiosity get the best of per.

The netter notices us from the corner of per eye, turns – and freezes.

This close, we can see ourselves reflected in per modified eyes. Small as a seahorse and bright as a clownfish, our tendrils of hair stream longer than our tails. Scales cover every inch of us, broken up only by our fins and our large, lidless eyes.

We can see the spark in per eyes, and we want to watch it die. We dart back, and the netter jerks forward. We swim to the side and the netter follows. Allowing the netter to keep up, we lead per deeper into the reef, further and further from per group and towards the drop-off.

The netter kicks after us, device raised to per face once more, creating flashes behind us. When we reach the edge of the reef, before it dips into the deep channel that runs across, we turn to face the netter, who drops per arms from per face hesitantly, worried that we may disappear, but we let per come closer. The netter reaches out a hand to us, and we scatter – forcing per to shift so that per back is to the sudden darkness of the drop.

The netter pulls back slightly, and we come back together. Per raises the device once more. Just before we swarm, another flash – but this time right in our eyes. For a moment there is nothing but white and then a psychedelic smear of yellow.

Our anger flares with the light and we surge forward with a snarl to clamp our jaws down on per fingers. Our vision clears in spots as per tries to shake free. Blood fills our mouths, hot and bitter. Per drops the device and it sinks straight down, hitting a rock and then falling into the drop-off.

We bite harder, pushing with all of our might, hoping to force per over the edge. We have only one wish: that the netter be caught by the current and swallowed by the ocean; that per bones snap the way per snapped the bones of our home. The current grows stronger, the ocean hungry for revenge.

The netter kicks and writhes as hard as per can to try and keep per balance, violently shaking per arms in horror. With one more frantic motion, one of us spins loose, flung over per shoulder with the force. Our jaws unlock from the netter's hands as we let out a cry, watching as the current grabs mer, consumes mer. We feel the white, cold heat of anguish hollow our stomachs and the sudden tearing emptiness of where mer consciousness was joined with ours. Mer is pulled into the deep, into the jaws of a barracuda.

The netter flees back through the reef. This time, we let per go as we stare into the abyss and try to dampen the ache of the hole that has now ripped through us.

One more piece of us, of home, taken away.

They come again. But these new netters are different. They come with spears.

The reef is still. We hold together, trembling amongst the rippling tentacles of the anemones, the colourful polyps of coral. We watch.

The light shifts and breaks, a fractured dance from the surface, and a dark form glides through the reef – these harbingers of death. A small clownfish trembles at the edge of the anemone growing from the base of our coral. Our curse weighs heavily on our shoulders.

And so, again, we follow as a netter breaks from the group. Spear tight in per grip, moving through the corals, searching. This netter, too, stops at damaged corals, but this one's touch is gentle along the colourless branches of the reef.

With a care that gives us pause, the netter slowly untangles a plastic bag that has twisted on a branch of staghorn, strangling what little life is left, and shoves it into the pocket at per waist. The staghorn's song eases, if only slightly. At every piece of litter, the netter stops and tucks it away into another pocket or pouch.

We continue to follow per into the tragically familiar section of reef. We had been avoiding coming back. We could not bear to see the damage, the growing number of thorns choking our palace.

Our hearts break clean in half at the sight before us. The reef seems built from the spines of starfish. Almost no coral is left untouched. It's hard to breathe, our gills failing to pull in water. Our heads spinning again.

The netter does not hesitate at the plague, instead only raises per spear and stabs it down into the reef. Anger flares again – hot like the blood we tasted from the last netter who tried to take our coral. We surge forward as the netter digs down . . . and hooks into the joint of a crown-of-thorns starfish, tearing its grip from the gnawed coral beneath.

We freeze.

The netter adds starfish after starfish to per bounty, ripping them from the coral. Only the corals' corpses remain.

After reaping a countless number from the seafloor, the netter moves to the shelf and pries each starfish from the bones of our palace. One by one, prying the plague from our true home.

If you look closely, you can see the tips of our tails turning white. You can see the pieces missing as our scales flake away, see our brittle fins tear as we move through the water.

We breathe with the reef, we bake with the reef, we bleach with the reef.

But though our colour is draining, though our home is crumbling, we are not dead.

Not yet.

The Deep

Far out in the ocean, where the water is as blue as spidering veins, it is deep. So very deep that no architect could fathom the number of floors it would take to fill the vast space between the mysterious ocean floor and the glittering surface waters. Or the array of steel and windows that could compare to the flawless gradient of periwinkle, azure, cobalt and midnight. It is here, in the deepest crevice, amongst fish that glow like embers between the broken glass, seagrass and shells, the merfolk dwell.

Here sits a mighty palace of coral and whale bone, with windows yawning between ribs, and ribbons of reef inlaid with mother of pearl and aluminium cans. Atop twisting spires flag plastic bags of yellow, grey and green. In the centre of the palace, the Merleader holds a concert to celebrate the fifth century of mer rule, audience twirling in a net of colours, captivated by the display. The merfolk turn, dive and twist, their jewel scales dazzling in the flurry of bubbles churning about them, lit up by the anglerfish in the depths. They wear capes of fishing-net torn from boat wrecks and hunters, and tangle themselves – fins jerking when they can no longer swim. Then they sink and spin free in a breath-snatching performance.

All watch, except for one. One who is lost in the knowable aquamarine waters of a lagoon, eyes captivated by a different display . . .

The young netters dally in the sweet, still shallows, ankles encased by the neap tide, and chase the dancing light refracting from the silver scales of the mer. They haven't noticed Ondine's inky hair rippling across the surface of the water behind the rocks, disguised by the coralline algae and the school of guppies drifting by. But the mer studies them. The vibrations had shivered along the lengths of mer fins – softer, safer than the nearby port harbour – drawing the mer to the small and quiet lagoon further along the shoreline.

The waters feel wild in their newness, even though the current is still, but the true wildness is the netterlings before mer. Ondine has always been fascinated by the things that dwell outside the ocean: the gulls that swim in the nothingness above, with their odd, wispy-soft scales and sharp beaks; the bristly beasts that run on all fours across the sand, tongues lolling stupidly as they chase their own excuses for tails; and the netters, with faces just like the merfolk. The netters are more curious – more disturbing – than any other. Instead of scales from hairline to tip, they have smooth, vulnerable skin wrapped in colours almost as vibrant as a healthy coral reef, and soft unstable limbs on which they trip and blunder. While Ondine observes, the ocean fills the gaps, its currents whispering the words of the worlds it has witnessed in its journeys inland, in the rivers and the skies.

Ondine winds free from the shelter of weeds, curling beside the rockpools where netterlings now slam and snatch and shake, disturbing crabs and starfish, prying barnacles from the pool walls. The netterlings are loud and clumsy. Destructive, but not yet dangerous – too young to bring ships spilling oil, killing reef after reef; too young to cast nets, pour waste and toss trash into the world beneath their feet. But bloodlust is in the netterlings' hungry eyes and groping hands, which plunge into the water with a cannon-fire violence. Guppies scatter and a hermit crab retreats into its shell, desperately clinging to the camouflage of its home but not quick enough to avoid a netterling's attention. The netterling collects it in per meaty hands, and the hermit crab lies still as practised death when per shakes and digs per pudgy fingers into the opening of the shell. The hermit's claws are not enough to save it. Ondine fights the burning in mer scaled chest as the crab is torn apart, and inches closer, ignoring the hot summer air drying out mer delicate skin. Still the netters do not notice – never notice much beyond what is convenient – and, tired, lie back up on the sand, resting only inches from the scattered corpses they created, and moving their mouths tirelessly – pointlessly to merfolk deafness – as small waves wash over them and then draw away.

When the sun begins to set, Ondine slips beneath the water again and swims in figure eights, mirroring the performers below, twisting, turning, catching the light in the last scales still holding their mercury sheen, but which are slowly becoming stained, diminished, from the slimy black death that continues to coat the ocean's surface.

A splash sends tremors through the water and Ondine smiles and allows mer tail to break the surface in a lazy wave. The water once more trembles along mer mercury scales as one of the netterlings steps back into the ocean, kicking and stomping in violent delight. Another flick of the mer tail and the netterling moves deeper, water to knees. The ocean swirls in approval, tide withdrawing to coax the small, bumbling legs.

Ondine raises mer head, smiling close-mouthed to hide small, pointed teeth. Slapping per hands together in glee per calls to another netterling, who has per hands buried in the sand, scraping a hole into the edge of the earth. Per looks over with curiosity, then per eyes widen as per clumsily pushes to per feet, tripping over the large pile of sand before sloshing into the water, gesturing wildly.

Ondine resumes mer dance, head above water, lips fixed in a soft, warm smile, bulbous eyes glittering. Arms out and afloat for balance, the netterlings wade after mer, deeper and deeper, until the water is at their chests. Ondine pauses, then unfurls mer long serpentine tail outwards, allowing the soft web of mer fins to tickle against the netters' scaleless bodies, shivering at the sensation.

Ondine doesn't flinch when the bigger netterling reaches forward to stroke mer, despite touching the throbbing red welts where scales have fallen away. Mer buries mer sharp teeth in mer lip and reaches out. The netters reach back, and with a tug they come along, smooth and trusting. Deeper . . .

A violent ripple crashes through the water and into the sensitive strands of Ondine's hair. The mer jerks back. Head snapping up, cold blood running still when mer sees a fully grown netter striding through the surf, face like a thunderstorm. Mer retreats in a flash, curling once more against the rocks, watching as the netterlings return to the grown netter's side and are ushered away. Ondine does not leave, even once the sun has set; instead mer rests, watching the shore through the murk of the waters.

Patient.

In the first hours of the morning the harbour is still. The water barely ripples, shielded from the ocean's pull, and the silhouettes of yachts and fishing boats look like jagged rocks against the navy sky.

The stillness allows Ondine to sense the toes entering the surf from along the shore. It takes barely any time for mer powerful tail to propel mer from the safety of the lagoon into the thick, brown waters of the harbour, where plastic catches in mer hair and cans cut at the exposed skin of mer tail where illness has touched. Ondine is too distracted to brush them away when mer raises mer head from the water and sees a lone shadow on the thin strip of sand.

Ondine has spent many hours here, and places like it, watching the netters and the four-legged beasts they keep enslaved on chains. Mer has tried to tally the number of times litter was left, carried by the wind and then dragged into the ocean's crying current. To be caught in the vacuum and sent out to sea. To sink into the depths. To be swallowed. To trap and deform. The merfolk have watched it build like a second layer of seafoam, pressing against the tide; watched it form toxic islands where gulls scavenge and die.

Now, a netter cringes at the seaweed left on the beach at low tide. Jumping and skittering, per tries not to let the soft, slimy material wrap around pers ankles, balancing on the point where the ocean kisses the shore. At first, Ondine mistakes the bumbling for that of a netterling. But as mer watches mer realises that the netter is an in-between – not netterling, yet not grown – a gangly, lurching creature, stumbling not from youth but the contents of the brown bottle that the netter is raising to per mouth.

Ondine has observed this performance many times. Eventually the bottle falls to the sand. Grasping at nothingness, in a delayed response, the netter stumbles, catches per footing, and then kicks the bottle with a force that dents the sand and watches as the vessel is claimed by the ocean – a hollow message.

The netter gives up on per wobbling legs and collapses, letting the tide tease around per sprawling body. The bottle is replaced by the slender stem of a – the word comes to Ondine from the crash of the next wave of the furious ocean – cigarette. Lighting up, the orange cherry glows through the darkness like a lionfish's warning stripes.

Flicking per wrist, the netter sends the butt arching through the air and it lands in the water, sizzling out. Another toxic offering. As the hours pass, per lights up another and another until there are enough butts to fill the stomach of a turtle and slowly starve it to death.

Snatching each one back from the current, Ondine clenches them in mer fist. Rage is a colour, a taste.

Enough.

The ocean churns, fuelling Ondine as mer surges forward, not caring about stealth, not caring about seduction. When the water becomes too shallow, mer drags merself on powerful arms. The splashes break the netter's haze, and horror and shock begin to register on per face as Ondine grabs the netter's foot and pulls.

The netter's mouth contorts, throat straining, veins bulging beneath the soft unprotected skin – the weaker evolution – and per struggles like a fish on a line, flopping grotesquely against the sand, resisting the pull of the ocean as it claims per. The struggle is admirable; shallow channels are gouged into the sand as per tries to anchor perself to the beach, but against the broad shoulders, powerful biceps and tail of the mer, the struggle is in vain.

Ondine shoves the cigarette butts clenched in mer fist into the netter's mouth. A savage grin splits Ondine's face as the netter chokes and splutters on the indestructible litter. Butts and ash dribble down per chin. There is no one around to hear and, with a single cloud blinking over the moon, the netter's contorted face disappears beneath the water. Bubbles fill with the screams and they become one with the seafoam.

All evidence of the struggle is washed away with the next deep breath of the ocean.

Ondine holds the netter under just long enough to put per to sleep, then, aware of per delicate lungs filling with water, allows the netter's head to break the surface. With mer arm firmly wrapped around the netter's chest, Ondine forces the liquid from the gangly in-betweener's mouth and per stirs, breath harsh and sour. But per does not wake.

Still alive.

For now.

Ondine begins to tow the netter out to sea, travelling slowly with the dead weight in mer arms and held back by the dangers of the ocean's surface: the netters' ever-expanding technology – the sonars that shout across the leagues and set the merfolks' teeth on edge. The merfolk have avoided detection, by rebuilding their kingdoms in the depths – by hiding in the darkness. Travelling this close to the surface requires Ondine's full attention, mer fins and strands of hair stretching out, seeking the subtlest of vibrations.

Ondine continues across the ocean until the first blush of dawn. With the sun's scorching kiss, the netter stirs in Ondine's arms and mer senses panic in the netter's muscles, feels the heat in the water as per body ejects more waste. The netter begins to struggle again, head rolling on per neck in confusion, in terror. Ondine tightens mer grip for a moment, then, with a grin, lets go.

The netter flounders, per head plunging below the water before per scrambles back to the surface in a desperate claw. Per twists wildly, spinning in circles, eyes hungry for land. Ondine can't contain the satisfaction burning in mer heart as the feverish light in the netter's eyes dies. There is nothing but water.

The netter's face contorts again, veins straining in per throat – trying to communicate in per motionless, redundant language.

Ondine bares mer sharp teeth, and the netter's face slackens and turns white when per also registers the scales covering Ondine's body from neck to fin. The netter's eyes flicker down to Ondine's tail, and per mouth trembles. Per violently slashes through the water, sending an arch of water into Ondine's face, but a film coats mer eyes, mer second eyelids, and mer just laughs low in mer chest and watches as the netter continues to frantically claw through the water. Ondine allows the netter to get three arm-lengths before plunging beneath the surface and then, shooting ahead with one powerful flick of mer tail, intercepts the netter and bares mer teeth, a dark triumph gleaming in black eyes.

The netter jerks to a halt and stares. Water wells in the lining of per lashes. Spreading out like a starfish, per floats on pers back. Ondine feels the sobs vibrating deep within the netter, but the netter's fear only fuels Ondine's hatred and mer grabs per once more. The netter doesn't struggle, resigned to fate, and the pair continue their journey out to sea.

※

The island is a speck at first – easily mistaken for a gull resting on the gentle waves.

At the sight of it the netter's heart starts pounding so hard in per chest Ondine feels it against mer scales. A fresh spill of tears rolls down the netter's sea-crusted cheeks and per begins to kick per legs, as if per could speed up progress.

When the island is only a mile away, Ondine lets go and the netter does not hesitate. Adrenaline rushes through per lanky limbs, giving per the strength to churn towards land. Ondine keeps pace.

The closer they swim, the clearer the island becomes and the slower the netter moves, until per falters.

Ondine watches the netter's face, wanting to see the realisation set in, to see per understand and shatter the same way Ondine has when watching the sick and dying of mer own kind grow around plastic rings and choke on the oil that gathers in their gills.

Decomposing bodies cover almost every inch of the island. The netter tries to scramble away, but Ondine grasps the netter's hair between webbed fingers, tangling it at the nape of the netter's neck in order to lock per head forward and force per to breathe in the harsh rot, the cloying bake of netters' flesh beneath the sun; to watch gulls peck at eyes and mouths; to see that beneath the gravemound of the netter's species, the island is made of plastic. Of chemical waste. Of trash.

Ondine lifts an arm and points towards the floating island.

The netter flinches, jerking free of Ondine's grip, turning per head and cowering. When there is no contact, the netter's eyes creep open and follow Ondine's pointed webbed, scaled fingers.

Per shakes per head violently, sobbing once more.

Ondine bares mer teeth, shoving the netter forward, per head submerging for a moment.

Spluttering, the netter moves toward the island, limbs wild, uncontrolled, as per drags perself through the water. Per pushes up, water sopping from per soaked clothes, and suddenly finds per feet on the micro-plastic that makes up the island's beach. Per slips, landing face-first in the armpit of a corpse and, on hands and knees, looks back to Ondine, pleading. But the mer has already slipped beneath the water and into the deep . . .

※

Far out in the ocean, where the water is as blue as spidering veins, it is deep. So deep that no submarine or drone could penetrate the crushing pressure; no netter could know what awaits within its dark crevices.

It is here that the merfolk bide their time, sharpening their spears of mother of pearl and shining their armour of aluminium cans.

There sits a mighty palace, scarred and vandalised, with plastic bags of yellow, grey and green caught in the ribs of a whale, choking the colour from the ribbons of reef.

In the centre of this palace, an army holds a rally. After five centuries of peace, the end of mer rule has been tainted by the suffering and deterioration of the merfolk as the netters plunged into the water and filled it with trash as if it had never been occupied. The Merleader has had enough. The ocean has had enough. The Merleader holds mer subjects captive as they whirl and jerk through the water in an evocative rage. The Merleader's audience mimics this language; their vicious war dance churns bubbles that glitter on the trash that is slowly killing them. Soon will come a day when the merfolk will rise from the deep in a violent gyre, through a flawless gradient of midnight, cobalt, azure and periwinkle.

All wait, except for one. One who draws the battle lines in trenches made of floating corpses. A warning, as their bodies are left to be swallowed by the sea.

Left to become nothing but seafoam on the waves crashing against the shore.

THE LAKE

In a dead, still world, a mer drifts.

In the murk, which grows thicker each passing day, almost nothing can be seen. Though what is worse, the murk or the emptiness that it hides, Odel does not know. So mer leans and looks up, through wide-set eyes, one on either side of mer head, never truly able to turn away from the aching nothingness below.

The moon watches from above, shining on the surface of the small lake, its bright light obscured only occasionally with the wisp of a cloud. In this light, Odel almost looks as mer once did – restored to mer true silvery self – the mud and missing scales refracting to perfection. The lake, too, is altered, and the eucalyptuses' shadows play in the moon's cast and almost resemble the life that once dwelled here.

Odel turns in slow circles and watches the colour of the surface change when the night is bleached by the sun. The world above comes to life and mer continues to turn. Every day the rays burn brighter, the lake grows smaller, and the water grows darker.

⊗

Odel's dance is broken by something shattering the surface. The ripples mimic life, and something like hope stirs in mer chest.

Mer darts up, head emerging, gills quivering in the fresh breeze, mer weed-like hair the only thing freeing mer from the poison of the stagnating water. The algae and mosquito-larvae-covered mane searches the sky for rain or birds. Only hot air greets mer, drying out the delicate skin of mer face beneath its brittle scales. Stomach twisting in disappointment and hunger, Odel begins to suck larvae from mer hair. When something flashes to mer left, mer twists, sinking lower, eyes locking on the gap between the gums. The bush shakes, and Odel's heart lurches. The whiskers on mer face vibrate. Mer hasn't seen another living creature in days.

A large, brown snout pokes from the underbrush. It snuffles. A long pink tongue spills out as it laps at an insect crawling across some dried eucalyptus.

Mer stomach twists again as the creature lets out a violent huff, shakes its great head, and pads over to the lakeshore.

It has been a while since Odel has seen a dog. The heat of the animal radiates through the air, causing mer whiskers to twitch. Odel slips beneath the still surface with barely a ripple, gliding below the shadow the dog has cast as it looks into the water. The dog cannot see Odel's shimmering body – half its size – circling slowly under the thick algae blanketing the lake. Mer waits for the dog to drink.

Just as its rough tongue breaks the surface, a larger shadow jerks the dog away before Odel can snatch it, drag it to the depths, tear at its flesh and suck the marrow from its bones.

Stomach rumbling, mer rises again through the broken water and sees a figure that almost looks like mer. Fear and anger seize in mer chest. Mer bares mer sharp little teeth in a silent snarl. Grasping the dog by the chain that circles its throat, the netter's skin glints with rivulets of water, and per drops a heavy weight from per shoulders and onto the ground.

Per pulls out a bottle the colour of the sea-glass Odel's miracle had once collected from quiet beaches and taken with them on their visits upstream. The per pours a stream of clear water for the dog to lap at. When it is satisfied, the netter too draws from the bottle, and, once empty, tosses it to the ground, where it rolls along the slight incline until it hits the water.

Dark water trickles in and through the neck until it is slowly swallowed.

At the bottom of mer lake, in a dark crevice that moonlight does not touch, is a treasure-trove. It holds Odel's collection of things that have appeared upon the lake and drifted to the bottom, like a second layer of mud. When the emptiness of the lake overwhelms mer, when the absence of the ocean chips at mer heart, when the pangs in mer stomach are unbearable, this treasure-trove is where mer comes. There are plastics of all colours, some thick and sturdy, others thin and suffocating; there is glass, broken and sharp, sometimes useful for removing dead scales. There are nails and hooks, rusted and toxic; firm rubbers, which are hard but satisfying to chew to keep the hunger pangs at bay; and shiny foils that look as though they've been made from the scales of the other merfolk – Odel's miracle – that once lived here.

And, now, a fresh bottle.

The river from the lake had once been bountiful, the moon's pull on the current so strong mer could ride it all the way to the ocean. Mer remembers the day the water stopped: when the world went still. Mer remembers when merfolk and fish turned upon one another, devouring each other until Odel was all that was left.

Odel has not heard the ocean's currents since the last rainfall – so many moons ago that Odel cannot recall exactly when. The memory is so worn that the feeling of being a part of something bigger than merself is starting to fade. Mer wishes mer could be with mer kin in the reefs, their miracles a collective mind, but mer wonders if the heat has destroyed them too.

A sudden vibration shimmers through Odel's hair and breaks mer reverie. Mer darts towards the surface to see a small creature writhing in the water. Mer streaks toward it before a moonlit glint has mer swerving at the last moment.

Slowly, carefully, mer winds back. Now, mer sees a small, metal hook protruding from the worm's body and smells the blood leaking into the water. Mer jaw aches with desire: with need. Reckless, mer swims closer, battling guilt and relief that the worm has no eyes to see its fate. Mer wraps a gentle claw around it: one thin, webbed finger stroking its length. With a violent pull, mer tears it off the hook, ripping it in half and then devouring it – without even a moment to savour this first morsel mer has eaten in days. But the worm does not sate; it only stirs mer hunger. Stirs mer anger. Odel dives to mer trove, snatching the fallen bottle, and darts back to the fishing line. Mer snarl churns in bubbles around mer as mer punctures the bottle onto the hook. *This is all that's left. You've taken it all.*

An all-consuming hatred burns through Odel as the fishing line is yanked back to the surface.

Odel rises to join the moon's gaze. Mer gills cry out at the hot, dry air. The dog's legs tremble and jerk: hunting, it seems, even in sleep. So does the netter – caught in dreams, Odel is sure, of building dams and flourishing settlements that the ocean had once sung about, while the world around per withers. Odel wonders if the netter ever has nightmares; if per knows that the earth where per sleeps was once a riverbed; if the per cares that while per gnaws on the bones of a bird cooked over per fire, per sits atop a graveyard.

For the first time, Odel wishes mer had legs. That mer could stride from the lakeshore, breaking the stillness of death that hangs like a snapped branch after a thunderstorm, rip the fishing-line from the netter's resting hands, and wrap it around per neck over and over again. Odel dreams of taking the hook, piercing the netter's lip, and dragging per into the lake to watch per struggle like a fish on a line till the air escaped per lungs. Then Odel would nibble at the netter's limbs, one by one, picking each bone clean and adding them to mer treasure-trove.

And yet, under the light of the moon, Odel does not transform. And the netter continues to dream, belly full as mer is sustained on a wish.

Odel watches until the burning sun rises. The air is the hottest it has been. Even the gum leaves on the trees hanging above the lake are ashen and curling.

The water is no better. It feels so thick that mer can barely find the energy to swim to its centre. Even in mer crevice, huddled beneath the trash, mer cannot find relief. Mer wonders how much more of mer lake will be lost to the sky today.

Something crashes through the water above. Every tendril on mer body – mer hair, mer whiskers, the wispy fins on mer tail – stands on end. Odel looks up at the shadow at the edge of mer lake, at the dog's plunging, oblivious paddle across the surface.

Odel grins, swims under the creature and gently brushes mer claws along its side, along the underside of its paws. Through the water mer can hear the dog's heartbeat, and mer can taste its excitement turn to fear as its paddling gets a little stronger, more urgent, and this time when Odel reaches up to it again, mer lets mer claws break through flesh. The coil of the blood in the water causes mer slit-like pupils to dilate. Mer isn't normally one to play with mer food but, angry and frustrated, mer slashes again and again and again. Urine permeates the water, but it barely makes a difference to the toxicity already festering in the lake.

Finally, when the smell of the blood is too much, mer reaches out and grabs the dog's kicking hind leg. Mer senses the yips of panic in the dog's throat as mer sinks mer teeth into it.

The blood is hot in mer mouth, and sweeter than anything mer has tasted in a long time. Odel rips a chunk of flesh from the dog's leg, then begins to drag the creature down: to drown it, to trap its leg between the rocks so mer can take mer time with every morsel.

But when another crash shatters through the lake mer loses mer grip, and the animal struggles free. The netter thunders through the water on per long legs, reaching for the dog. Odel snatches at the dog's legs again, pulling hard, but the netter gets an arm around the animal's midsection and hauls it from the water. Odel's strength is no match for the netter's.

The netter carries the panicking dog to shore, tears strips from per green shirt, and wraps them around the dog's leg. Per soothes it with long, gentle strokes.

Odel can still taste the dog as mer circles the lake, one eye on the litter-covered ground below, the other on the sky. One eye on destruction; one eye on salvation.

Mer waits.

A flickering orange against the dusk coaxes Odel back to the surface. Mer is slow and sluggish, the water still feverish from the light of the day. There is no relief when mer head emerges; the air is parched. Out of one eye, mer can see the netter and dog around a hungry fire. It seems larger than the night before. It has its own gravity, roaring and pulling all moisture from the world around it. The small space feels hotter than it was even in the sun: thick and cloying and hazy.

The netter dozes. A thick trail of liquid spills from a dark glass bottle tilting in per hand, as if it too is being called by the fire.

Odel feels the whoomph, as the burnt air blows through mer hair like vibrations through the water. There is a flare: blinding and sudden. The raging fire crackles, spits, splits, and showers across the bush. Scrub catches and flames race from the base of the eucalyptuses to their tops.

The netter stirs from either the sound or the heat, or perhaps the pressure. The whites of per eyes are bright as the eyes of the moon. Per scrambles to per feet and lunges for the bags per left leaning against a tree: the bags which have already been devoured by the flames.

The dog too has jolted awake, panicked, its large nostrils dragging in the toxic waste pluming up up up.

The fire is dancing, joyous, infectious as it leaps from tree to tree. Odel is transfixed, watching until the netter snatches the dog up into per arms and, turning, crashes back through the bush against the fire's path. Mer watches as other creatures – scaled, four-legged, round, spiney – pour from the underbrush and plunge into the lake. Masses of singed fur fall from the trees, eucalyptus leaves still clenched in the creatures' paws. Odel watches the surface of mer lake steam, and feels mer flesh begin to simmer beneath mer scales.

Odel plunges, flees from the heat, as deep as mer can go – to the crevice – mer horror reflected back at mer from every one of mer treasures.

The fire burns on. For how long Odel does not know; the dark smoke blocks out the sun. But mer is not worried – for the first time in many moons, food is abundant. Odel rips off melted quills and singed fur and gnaws on burnt flesh. Over moons, when the flesh is finished, Odel will gnaw on the bones.

Mer tastes hope. But only for a moment.

The smoke above grows thin. The first shard of light cuts through Odel's lake and mer finally ventures to the surface.

The world is black and shredded – tilted and collapsed and still smoking. No green remains and nothing rustles with life. Even the algae on the surface has shrivelled up.

The world above is now just as stagnant as mer world below.

One day again, under the moon's watchful eye, the stillness is broken. A clawed hand rises from below, and then an arm, a stomach, a fin. The night's gaze is met with the glassy, sightless eyes of the mer. Life around the lake has begun to bloom again, with starts and spurts of green. A death shroud of algae covers mer scales, larvae borne from mer rotting flesh.

THE BOAT

Once

Once, a ship had been caught in the swelling waves as a thunderstorm crashed across the seas. Lightning crackled through the sky, brightening the black waters to reveal an outcrop of jagged rocks almost invisible in the darkness.

From the rocks Unzel commanded, songs pouring from mer lips in the rhythm of the current that ran through mer veins. Mer voice beckoned over the screaming wind, clear as the bell that snapped from the crow's nest and rich as the lands the netters sought to pillage, stirring the seas into a gyre and capturing every soul on board the doomed ship.

Unzel watched the netters try to save their vessel from the maul of the ocean, and danced along to their guttural cries, encouraging the cacophony.

Mer sang to protect the merfolk's palace just beyond the drop-off, and mer took great pleasure in mer service.

Lightning struck again, and Unzel's golden scales blazed like the rising sun. The ocean churned in satisfaction as the netters' eyes glazed when they beheld mer curled on mer throne of stone. Unzel's song drowned out the crash of thunder that followed, and the netters' ship began to tilt as it followed the croon of the song and towards mer throne.

Unzel dived into the depths before the vessel made contact. Pieces of the ship fell around mer, like sparkling red flares, before trickling to the seafloor. Mer carefully avoided the ship's giant nets, slicing them with the sharp fins of mer tail. The rest of the vessel began its descent with a symphony of cracks, sinking like a blue whale. Then, just as the last breath left the netters' lungs, and before their legs could turn to tails, Unzel cut her song. And when the ship settled with a cloud of sand on the ocean floor, Unzel returned to mer rock, triumphant.

With each rise and fall of the sun, Unzel's collection grew till the floor beneath mer became more graveyard than seabed.

But mer voice did not wane.

Now

Now, Unzel no longer has much use for the rocks from which mer was born.

With submarines that can travel deep below the water and the ships above allowing netters to remain safely tucked in their metal bowels, mer voice can no longer reach susceptible ears. Instead, the ships stay their course and their sonars and nets cut through the mysteries of the ocean.

Unable to protect their city from the probing of the netters, the merfolk abandoned the palace beyond the drop-off. Unzel was left alone, tethered to the rocks that bore mer. For if Unzel wanders too far, the Merleader's song, and the slap of the water on stone that had called mer into being, would unravel. For Unzel had not been born as merfolk were, but made.

Now, Unzel nests in the rusting skeleton of mer final victory – a ship sunk at the edge of the drop-off that leads to the abandoned palace. Once a graveyard, it now sprawls with life. Barnacles bloom from the hull, which is spotted with oysters and bright corals in lilac, periwinkle and peach. Crabs scuttle across the sand, fish weave between vibrant plants, and a grey reef shark glides through schools of angels, blue tang, wrasse and snapper.

The fish understand Unzel but often ignore mer, sensing something unsettling about mer golden scales and curved, netter-like ears. To them, mer is ancient and mysterious, more ocean than sea creature.

Sometimes, the ocean's current brings Unzel tales of the other merfolk – how they thrive in their new homes in the depths, without mer. Unzel welcomes the stories, sustains merself on them despite their bitter aftertaste.

Mer watches the surface from below, caressing the harpoon and bullet wounds that litter mer body. Not all ship crews fell prey to Unzel's song. Those who broke free of mer song fought back, then fled the grasp of the ocean. The netters sang their own tales on their ships' bows: of the monster waiting for them in the depths of the sea.

The swarm of glinting fish obscures the surface above. Beyond the surface, the refracting sunlight and the seafoam crashing against the rocks distort the gulls and the clouds in the sky. Occasionally, large shadows from the impenetrable ships swallow everything in sight.

When Unzel can bring merself to the surface and rest on mer rock, mer sings only to the gulls. They do not seem wary; instead they are drawn to the way mer glints in the sunlight. Sometimes, if they find mer song worthy, they will gift mer with shiny things from beyond the ocean: mirrors and forks and delicate golden chains. The ocean sings as Unzel inspects the objects – a symphony of currents that has journeyed to the sky, to the rivers and back to the ocean – and it whispers to mer the names it has learned and the stories of those who walk in the waters like they own them. Unzel listens to their stories and decorates merself in the chains, necklaces and bracelets, which remind mer of the cuffs of bones merfolk wear to distinguish their miracles.

The seabirds wear jewellery, too. Their legs are clamped in plastic, as if in the claws of a crab. They come in smaller flocks each year, their bellies filled with rubber butts and the fat they snatch from netters' hands. Lazy and lethargic, many gulls can no longer leave the beaches to hear mer songs.

Today no birds have come on the sky's currents – no gifts of foil or coins or needles – so Unzel sings to the empty horizon until a shadow appears on its line.

At first mer thinks it's a gull or perhaps even a dolphin. But as the shadow grows larger, rage forms a fist around mer heart. Unzel knows exactly what it is – a ship. Even rusted and clunky, it is still smoother, sleeker, harder than the wooden ships mer sank centuries ago. It cuts through the water like a dorsal fin.

Unbidden, Unzel's voice pours from mer throat in a song so old mer had almost forgotten it. The ocean crashes in response and storm clouds gather, but the bow of the ship slices straight through.

Mer flees the rock and descends to the sunken crow's nest. Mer song continues, and the entire reef stills as all life retracts, holding its breath, waiting for the ship to pass – watching as the ship's great net drags behind it.

The waters warm, the eggs hatch, and the boats chug steadily above. After a few catches, those in her reef no longer notice that the schools have become thinner and thinner.

Every tendril on Unzel's golden head and tail trembles with the reverberation of the motors disturbing the surface, and with the churning of the fish from the water. Mer is almost numb to the sensation, half-deaf to the currents of the ocean. Anger, once hot in mer chest, succumbs to powerlessness when mer realises mer cannot stop the machines as they leach life after life. Mer bones ache to go back to the throne of jagged rock and from there sink the ships and watch as the netters drown and jerk for air on the ocean floor, the way the fish flounder on the decks of the ships.

Instead, Unzel watches and waits.

⊗

One day the boats don't come.

Nor the next.

Nor the next.

And the day after, the sky turns red.

The boats return, a fleet of all shapes and sizes, clustered together like a school of guppies upon the muddy, black waves. Unzel has never seen so many on the water at once. But the ships do not drag their nets. In fact, they do nothing. Mer swims beneath them, following the path of their shadows into the deeper sea, swimming far enough away that the netters do not see mer golden head when it emerges.

The thick grey air seeps poisonous into Unzel's gills and the sun burns like an all-seeing eye through the fiery haze. Upon the ship decks, netters crouch and stare at the burning shore, mouths covered with shirts, gas masks, and another odd materials, faces dark and deformed so that they almost remind mer of the fish that lurk in the sea's darkest depths.

Unzel follows the netters' stares, blinking mer double eyelids to clear the ash. Mer sees giant plumes of smoke blooming from the earth and into the sky. The flames leap between the gnarled white branches of the eucalyptus trees and glow like the bioluminescence that flowers on the seafloor. The flickering races forward, leaving only skeletal black branches behind. Further off, on the thin shore, those without a boat huddle together against the onslaught.

The searing colour is a crackling roar the ocean knows well. Its currents whisper news of the raging fires that grow even larger as the lakes and dams where water once fell can no longer be reached, the air dry and dead.

The boats remain the next day and the next, a floating cemetery. The gulls have disappeared from the sky.

At first, the netters are quiet. Words shared only in whispers, arms wrapped around each other and water leaking from their eyes as they wait out the danger flickering on the shoreline. Occasionally they eat and toss trash carelessly into the ocean, scattering the silver schools below as the rubbish sinks down to the reef. Some try drinking the sea water, and Unzel delights when their bodies reject it. After running out of options on board, the netters begin to expose their bodies and relieve themselves into the ocean in dark brown streams.

Soon Unzel can no longer observe from below, the surface black and so thickly marbled with ash that it begins to eclipse the reef. As the land continues to burn, the sky a glowing mirror of the devastation on the ground, the netters pace across their decks, or toss things back and forth from one boat to another. Unzel too grows restless with discomfort, spending more time on the surface, hidden in the jagged rocks, the hot acrid water there pouring into mer gills and choking mer. But Unzel cannot resist the opportunity to observe, and with the air so thick, mer doubts they would notice if mer swam right beside them.

Some netters with bigger boats begin to leave – burning their fuel, adding new shades of grey to the tapestry of the sky – and mer follows them as they try the next cove and the next. Eventually mer returns, more interested in the smaller boats that have no choice but to stay.

It doesn't take long for the netters' fear to fracture into anger. Some netters are pushed overboard. Some jump ship, seeming desperate for water or food. Larger boats – those with the sickly yellow sides and flashing lights that look like the crackling fire – return to tug the smaller boats away.

And still the fire rages on.

The night is blacker than it has ever been when the last of the lingering boats is tugged away, but it is through the deep haze of sunrise when Unzel sees something new emerge across the horizon.

This boat is the smallest yet: bright green and white and wooden, reminiscent of the long-ago vessels that Unzel found pleasure in singing to their wrecking. At first mer thinks the boat is empty, perhaps having snapped from a rope off one of the wharves further up the coast. Unzel approaches with hesitant strokes, and then brushes the end of mer long tail along the belly of the boat. The boat lurches in response to mer touch and mer jerks underwater when a small head pops over the side.

The netterling is small, young. Per hair, once blond, is matted with soot, and per face is crusted with sea salt, sand and ash. A trembling hand reaches down to the water right above Unzel's submerged head, swirling through the black, trying to clear the surface to bring a mouthful to per lips.

The netterling retches and sags against the edge of the dinghy, eyes shut and face red, though whether from exertion or the sun's reflection off the water, Unzel isn't sure.

Curling beneath the small vessel, Unzel comes up on the opposite side to peer over the edge. The first thing mer notices is the netterling's legs, thin and knobbly and buckled beneath per slumped body. The netterling's feet are bare, caked as black as per hair, and streaked with deep red from cuts between per toes.

There is not much else in the boat. A bucket filled with sand and waste. An empty box. A scattering of foil wrappers. A raggedy-looking animal with split fur and bulging white fluff, which the netter clings to per chest. A torch rests at the netterling's feet.

Something soft and alien sinks in Unzel's chest. Something like sympathy.

The sun falls beneath the horizon, and the only light is the angry orange still burning across the shore. The netterling jerks in the boat and the stark torchlight illuminates the cloud of smoke that seems to have permanently settled on the water. The light hits the netterling's face: it is gaunt, skeletal and afraid. A loud crack comes from the shore as a tree gives way to destruction.

One of the few species of merfolk gifted with hearing above water, Unzel listens to the deep rumble from the netterling's stomach, and the shuddering sobs from per throat. Unzel has never heard anything like these delicate and congested cries – only the death cries of poachers and explorers.

The netterling turns inwards and crawls on per knees to rustle through the wrappers, only to find the hollow crackle of nothingness. Per shoulder blades protrude and remind Unzel of the clipped wings of a gull. Another sob rips from per small chest – harsher, older than the others.

Halfway through the night, the light goes out and a small wail escapes the netterling's lips, before per sinks into a jerking, jagged sleep.

In the early hours of dawn, Unzel wedges the boat firmly into the rocky outcrop, using mer tail to protect it from the ocean's current. The netterling jerks awake, and per eyes immediately find the pile of seaweed resting at the bottom of per boat. Per head snaps around, but Unzel is well hidden between the rocks.

Unzel doesn't know what possessed mer to retrieve the seaweed from the seafloor, or to grasp the boat before it was pulled further out into the open ocean. Mer has never before led a boat to mer rock for any reason besides destruction. But watching the netterling squat over the bucket rather than the ocean, before crumpling back into fitful sleep, has shaken something loose in Unzel's chest.

Mer watches as the netterling prods the slimy mass at per feet, picking up a strand and sniffing delicately before taking a hesitant bite and then cringing. But the rumbles in per stomach win out and per almost chokes on the seaweed as it slides down per throat. Brightness lights the netterling's eyes as per washes the sustenance down with an acrid swallow of sea water. Then per spreads out along the base of the boat, rubbing per swollen stomach, and falls into a light doze.

Unzel remains in the rocks, watching the netterling, the burning shore and the horizon, with mer tail curled protectively around the boat. Mer ignores the plea of mer gills as the filthy water stirs against them, mer chest rattling almost as loudly as the netterling's.

⊗

In the afternoon the wind changes, throwing every piece of debris and waft of smoke directly into the ocean. The netterling's heavy breathing turns to racking coughs as per weak lungs struggle.

Gasping, the netterling pulls off per filthy shirt and dunks it into the water, stirring as deep as per can to rinse off and avoid any excess filth. Then per pulls it around per mouth and knots the sleeves against the base of per skull to hold it in place.

The netter stares out to the horizon, arms wrapped around per knees, hair whipping across per eyes in the hot wind, and the heavy wet fabric puffing rhythmically with every breath.

The sun rises and falls once more but no boats come, and any remaining spark in the netterling's eyes fades. With every rolling wave, the dinghy grates against the rocks, the wood splintering with each swell.

It only takes one large exhale of the ocean for the first crack to splinter the boat's side. Water surges into the dinghy and the netter jumps to per feet, boat lurching dangerously, threatening to capsize. Eyes wild, per tips the nearly full waste bucket into the ocean and begins to scoop the water out of the rapidly filling boat in short, frantic, pointless motions.

Unzel keeps mer tail wrapped tightly around the vessel, but the crack continues to fracture like a bolt of lightning, the water filling the boat faster than the netterling can scoop. The only thing stopping the boat from sinking is Unzel's grip. When the water reaches the netterling's mid-thigh, per gives up and drops the bucket.

Ripping the shirt from per face, per leaps from the boat and plunges into the water.

Unzel unwinds mer tail, slides from the rocks into the ocean, and takes the first clean breath of water in hours. Mer sees the netterling's weak and clumsy strokes reaching for the receding surface as per begins to sink. Bubbles churn from the netterling's throat as per screams and chokes.

A deep, old instinct awakens within Unzel, and a different song spills from mer throat. Mer sings the song of the merfolk. Sings of the way the light refracts through the waves, the way fins glide through the water. A song of blessed shell charms that once hung on the bones of the front door of the palace. A song of young hatching from an egg, of life blooming between the corals, the seaweed, the foam.

Unzel sings a song that hasn't been sung in centuries: a song of creation.

After

After, perched upon mer throne of jagged rock, Unzel gazes at the shore. The air has cooled and the coastline is no longer a line of charred bones, but instead is lush and green. Greener than it had ever been. The sky is smokeless and filled with gulls, their coloured tags flashing in the warm yellow sunlight.

There is nothing left to show of the days when the sky was red and the world was burning.

Even the large, clunking, impenetrable boats have returned, dragging their great nets and schools of silver fish that are left to suffocate on the boats' cold, hard decks – as they've always been.

Unzel is no longer alone. Beside mer, on the rock that bore them both, the once-netter rests. The fingerling's tail is long and silver and sweeping, entwined with Unzel's. Songs fall from their lips, songs of loss and love and rebirth. The gulls swoop and dance to their cadence.

Their voices do not wane. Together, a miracle.

THE AQUARIUM

My entire body is burning. Every caress of smooth, thick water feels like the sting of an anemone. My claws scratch at my scales, rip them off, desperate for relief. I can barely see, my eyes blinded by a murky film, despite my adipose eyelid. My black deep-sea hair is brittle and breaking, as are the tendrils that flow from the fins of my tail. Unable to sense the vibrations through the water – now barely a rippling echo – I am truly blind. I have not heard the guidance of the ocean's song in many moons.

My captor either does not care or does not understand – or perhaps does not care to understand. Per just continues to wave per arm, trying to conduct me the way the Merleader speaks to the seas. An imposter, a shadow, trying to create per own empire within glass walls.

The netter has long learnt to keep out of my reach.

I had only done it once, when I was still strong. I had hoped they would find me too wild to tame, and release me. The netter had dived boldly down to the pool floor, fish in hand, wide smile magnified by the water's refraction, and met me face-to-face. The water caught in my gills at the sight of those odd eyes with their colours and their whites, at the limp hair that reached only upwards and felt nothing.

Per held the dead fish, and the scent of its rotting flesh came in sharp waves from the current created by per arms. What was left of the sensitive strands of my hair shrivelled inwards and away. My captor gestured up towards the surface, tried to coax me from the bottom of the pool, to soothe me with treats as if I were one of per bumbling young, instead of a creature older than the continent itself. But my eyes were clouded with chemicals, and so per could not, would not, see the anger there.

The captor's touch had been gentle at first, a caress against my scaled arms, but per became more insistent when I failed to react, to take per offering, to rise to the surface with per before the last bubble of air released from per weak lungs.

I watched the moment when per gave up and accepted per need to return to the surface, the way per arm stopped moving as per rose. I grabbed per delicate forearm. The captor's eyes lit up with joy, but then quickly turned to fear as per stared into my large black eyes. Per felt the unmatched strength of my webbed, clawed hands, hardened from centuries of propelling myself through the ocean.

Per tugged, then struggled, wriggling like a fish on a hook. My claws breached the first layer of skin, then the second. Just as the last breath tore out from per throat in a torrent of bubbles, I let go, and per thrashed back to the surface.

They starved me for days afterwards. The captor returned with others, weapons strapped to their hips, poles in their hands, their eyes cold.

Now, when I fail to respond – when my tail thrashes to escape the chemicals eating away at me – a rod cracks down hard across the scales on my back. The sensation almost relieves the itchy skin beneath, but only for a second. They hit me in places that do not leave obvious marks, but enough of my once beautifully iridescent scales have flaked off and sunk to the smooth, colourless floor – lifeless, like the pungent, rotten, silver fish that get tossed to me in an attempt to ingratiate me when their punishments do not work.

The next strike lands across my webbed hands. They yank my weakened arms from where they are wrapped around me and splay them against the ledge of the pool. The pole comes down with a harsh snap. A screech rips from my throat, a plea in a language that is only spoken beneath the waves. My claws instinctively swipe out, but my hands can barely flex with the throbbing.

Sometimes I wonder what stopped their gentle coaxing. Is it because I do not have a throat like theirs? That I am not a siren who sings them into assurance? That they cannot read the flick of my tail and the twist of my shoulders? Or was it that moment of connection, the window into each other's eyes, that revealed to them an intelligence that made me seem all too familiar to them, and no longer a simple sea dog?

But my ribcage now protrudes from the small soft scales of my belly and I am too weak to resist. I come when called and I learn their routine. I rise and dive and twirl in this achingly-small, colourless imitation of the ocean. Fully extended, the tip of my tail – five times longer than my torso – touches the smooth, cold ground, and the tips of my fingers reach the rippling surface. The only time I can stretch out is when I twist through the air, arch across the surface of the water, fly up and down, and soar through the centre of five rings – careful, so careful not to touch the edges.

Once they are satisfied with my performance, I receive the rotten fish – the fruits of my labour – and they tie bright strands, like soft coral, through my hair, shine my remaining scales, and glue shells to the front of my chest. The netters try to dress me like the garish image of a mer-tailed red-headed netter, who flies from all the posts and hangs above the pool. A myth come to life – a myth sung by sirens and cackled at by those of us below. The first ever in captivity. The first ever seen since the stories told by their sea-crazed ancestors centuries ago.

The netters come in five tides a day.

It's the same every time.

The five dolphins begin the show, circling the pool with just a hint of their dorsal fins above the surface, building the anticipation. With each lap of the pool, they rise just a little bit higher, and just as the audience is getting restless, the dolphins launch from the water and flip in the air.

I can feel the netters' cheers through the concrete, their stomps reverberating and disturbing the water. The dolphins echo curses to each other as they descend, and then rise once more and begin to dance. Protruding upright they wiggle in a circle, waving their fins at the audience – an obscene spectacle from my view below – flippers wagging like a dog's tail. They move outwards, their tight circle expanding – and that's my cue.

I spin through the water like a hurricane and explode up into the centre, thrashing the water with my long muscular tail to hold myself upright in the air. I don't look towards the audience, but I know they have gone wild. I can feel their feet stomp so strongly against the bleachers that it ripples down into the water.

I hold myself in place, the lower half of my tail trembling as it beats frantically to keep me upright, until I see one of our captors give the signal. I relax every muscle and drop like a stone. With barely a moment to take in a breath of water, I must rise again as the centrepiece of the dolphins. We hold our bodies upright, my arms spread wide as if to embrace the audience, and do another lap of the pool. We sink below once more, and I stay at the bottom of the pool and wait. The dolphins begin their tricks, flipping through the air, catching balls on their snouts, allowing our captors to ride on their backs.

The audience is restless; the water churns with it. Just as the excitement reaches its peak, as it crests, as the dolphins perform their final arc, I rise.

Muscles coiling, I leap. Fully extended, I am a rainbow stretched across the horizon, my scales a dazzling lightshow in the mid-afternoon sun. The dolphins join me, diving in perfect synchrony, and my long tail ripples behind us like an afterimage.

The water thunders with savage excitement. When the dolphins slip away with one final wave, I'm left alone, trapped under the weight of the netters' stares.

I face my captor, who stands on the landing in the centre of the pool, with the water at my waist and the ends of my hair fanning out around me. This time, I can't stop my eyes from flicking to the audience. Their arms wave in the air. They're desperate for my attention. It takes all of my self-control not to lift my scaled arms, to wave back at them, equally desperate, to scream Let me out! Let me out!

My captor gives the signal – a quick twitch of per fingers – and I lift the end of my tail from the water in a large, lazy wave. With another gesture, the large hoops hanging above lower into position, and we begin the next routine. Three sets of jumping and hauling my tail through hoops, without touching the edges.

By the final set, I am tired. On the last hoop, my thoughts fill with the relief of diving back into the water. My tail weakens and my long fins knock the circle.

Fear is sharp and sudden as I sink into the water and, when I emerge again, I meet my captor's red and angry face. My scaled hands tremble. With another sharp gesture, I prepare for the next act.

A netter passes my captor a large green ball. Spinning it atop one of per fingers, per announces something to the crowd and then throws the ball to me. Lifting my exhausted tail, I twist it into a large loop, hold this pose, then pull myself along the water, allowing the ball to pass through me.

Every netter in the crowd leaps to their feet.

I throw the ball back, and my captor returns it immediately. I have to move quickly to create the hoop. We do this over and over, me contorting more and more each time, until, finally, I miss. My tail cramps and slaps the water.

This time, I do not look up to see the anger in my captor's face, but I dart to fetch the ball, and, hands trembling once more, I throw it back – smacking per in the face. Per stumbles with the force and drops the ball.

My stomach twists.

The dolphins return for the finale. I am already panting, chest rising and falling, trying to draw air through my gills, and my tail feels like a sunken ship. But still, I haul it from the water. I twist it, not into one loop, but two, straining every inch of muscle, pulling my spine. As each dolphin leaps through, the structure trembles, and my eyes feel as if they're going to burst. As soon as the fifth dolphin disappears beneath the surface, I dive straight down.

Just before my head hits the bottom, I arc back and shoot straight up. I feel their screams as I soar over the water in a glistening backflip, then disappear once more.

I take the water deep into my gills. It's over.

There is a grate at each end of the bottom of the pool: one for me and one for the dolphins. They do not speak to me, do not acknowledge me. I sense their fear, their uncertainty. Bred in captivity – all but one – they have not seen my kind before. In their eyes, I am more like those above the surface than those who dwell below. In this artificial world, I don't belong.

The grate for the dolphins opens and they glide through, returning to their enclosure.

My grate stays shut.

Fear is still thrumming through me, my mistakes burned into my brain.

When the dolphins' grate closes and my grate still does not open, I know that they wait for me above.

I return to the surface. The bleachers are empty now. The only netters at the pool are my captors, waiting for me, arms crossed on the platform in the centre. I want to move slowly, to take my time, but I know that will only agitate them more. When I reach them, one crouches low to look at me. Per eyes are a pale blue, almost the same colour as the icecaps that had seemed to look on when I lost my freedom. I am wondering what per thinks of my eyes, if the all-black scares per, when suddenly per smacks my face hard.

The force against my scales cuts per palm open. Per blinks, looks down at the blood welling from per lifeline, as if surprised. Per looks at me, and for a moment I feel that connection again, see per expression shift, searching for something in my steady, sad gaze. Per mouth opens, as if to speak, but at the last minute per presses per lips together as if remembering that there is no point. Looking from my face to per hand, per shakes per head. Then, per slowly swirls per hand through the water to rinse away the beading red, pushes to per feet and waves per arm once more.

The connection breaks. Cheek throbbing, heart twisting, I return to the centre of the pool.

Per picks up the ball and begins to throw.
We do not stop until the sun sets.

⊗

When I am allowed to return to my tank, I spill
from the tunnel to the bottom where there is a cave
just large enough for me to hide.

There are no fish in my tank – they didn't want
to tempt me. But I am never truly alone. Netters
press their faces against the glass and ogle me at all
times. Even at night, they come and sleep beside
the glass, for a magical night with a myth.

I don't mind having the tank to myself, though
I am still the only one of my kind trapped in here,
dangled like a trinket.

⊗

I was alone the day they found me, alone but for
the ocean's encouraging currents. They entertained
me on my journey through the ice-capped southern
waters, with the songs of the sirens. My kind
generally do not wander so far from home, but I
was curious to leave my miracle and travel the seas.

A netter expedition had been on the ice that day,
snatching penguins and clipping them with tags

– just like the tag now pierced through my fin. The ocean had tried to warn me. The currents worked against me, as dense as the water in the deepest crevices, but I had been distracted, avoiding the attention of a lion seal when I passed their ship, and someone saw me through the rounded glass. It did not take long for word to spread, for the hunt to start. And though I fought, I was helpless against the darts that pinched my underarms, where the flesh is soft and unprotected by scales. The darts sent sleep through me.

I woke in the pool. Every day I was poked and prodded, parts of me cut away. The tendrils on my tail and fins, my hair, my scales, my flesh, my blood. Then, when they'd taken enough of my body, they starved away the rest so I could fight no longer.

Now, every night, after being worked to exhaustion with no food and new bruises kissing my skin, I hide as best I can in my cave. I curl my tail around myself, wrap my arms around the throbbing wounds, and hope for the day my body gives out. I listen with the tendrils I have left to the empty, lifeless waters.

With every rise of the sun, it starts again. The dolphins do their circuits, their jumps. I do my leaps, my hoops. We play ball.

Day after day, the dolphins ignore me. They echo sounds of encouragement to each other and force trills that the netters mimic through their laughter. The dolphins dance to their own shadow orchestra – a song that is slowly unravelling the threads of my sanity.

So, instead, I write my own song. As I dive and whirl and twist my tail, I sing in ancient rhythms. I tell the story of an earth-shattering quake that cracked the ocean floor, of the first kiss between molten core and sea water that birthed the first Merleader. How with the swell of the first mer song – a harmony with the ocean – continents rose to the surface, fish crawled to land and grew legs. I sing about how they forgot us.

With the language of the deep echoing through the water, I sing of the vast blue endlessness. I sing of the eroding coasts, the paling reefs, the melting icecaps. Of the merfolk's palaces and cities, of our miracles that make up our families – generations living in one whalebone home. I sing of our colours and diversity, how we reach every body of water across the world, connected by the water's cycle from the ocean into the sky and back down. I tell the dolphins about their home.

As we weave in and out of the water, I feel the echoes of another song intertwining with mine and reverberating off the glass cage. The oldest of the dolphins tells of being pulled from the ocean, being passed from glass prison to glass prison, being forced to breed, and of calves taken away. The dolphin sings about slowly becoming blind until it was impossible to learn any new routines, and about becoming my sideshow.

At the end of the song, the next dolphin begins a new song – of far-off prisons, where the captors hand-raised the dolphins then ripped them from their surrogate pods to perform elsewhere. And so the dolphins begin to ache for the world they were never a part of, and the world I will never see again. Together we long for freedom, and the water no longer feels empty.

Every twist and turn and jump and trill is a song we sing for each other: our own private performance.

As the days burn hotter, the shallow water of our pool warms. It's harder to breathe, harder to sing. The oxygen burns away in the steady heat. The dead fish we are fed after every trick are hot and slimy.

During practice, the netters' rods crack more often, hard enough to bruise the flesh beneath my scales, to make the dolphins flinch in sympathy. Hard enough that the dolphins' echoes of encouragement extend to me. Hard enough that when I look into their eyes, once hollow with compliance, they now reflect my anger, my loss. Hard enough that we don't forget.

Today the sun is so hot that every moment I am above the surface, the water immediately evaporates from me. By contrast, the netters have water running down their faces, pooling in the pits of their arms. But the seconds I am beneath the water aren't long enough for me to even draw water into my gills.

My head is spinning.

I fumble.

The show ends, but I do not bother to swim down to my grate. Instead I float on my back, my gills straining to draw in the oxygen from the hot water, and I wait for the rod.

But this time, the dolphins turn back. This time they stay.

And this time, when the rod comes down, the eldest dolphin leaps, and its snout clamps down hard on the captor's hand. Per face twists in a scream and per tries to rip free, but the dolphin's tight grip jerks per down, and per slips into the pool. I smell the blood as it disperses in the water, a red wisp curling from the dolphin's jaw.

Other captors run over, throats straining with anger. They try to pry the dolphin's jaw open. One smacks the dolphin hard on its snout. Outraged, the other dolphins surge forward, snapping at per hand. The captor falls back in terror as the dolphins turn to per companion and bite down on per arms, per legs.

Before I can move to help – before I can wrap my long tail around the captor's waist and drag per to the bottom of the pool, where I can watch the last of per air explode from per lungs and see the life fade from per eyes – more captors come. This time, they carry weapons that shoot sleep, and a dart hits me right between my eyes. The last thing I see is the dolphins being shot, their grips releasing as they begin to float motionlessly. Their eyes hollow once more.

When I wake, I am alone in my tank. The water is empty. No netters press against my glass or sleep on the ground beyond. Days pass, and I am not disturbed. The only sign of my captors are the dead fish that sink down from the surface.

But when I am finally beckoned, when the grate opens to lead me to the pool, no one answers my echoes; no one shares my song.

There are no dolphins, just me.

WRITING FROM BELOW

Samantha Amy Mansell's *Mer* is a collection of watery fables for toxic times. They are stories of bodies changed, of rapidly shifting environments. Reefs, oceans and lakes are overfished, stuffed with plastics, thrumming with sonic disturbance from extractive industries, and inland lakes are thick with the settled ash of raging fires. Merfolk trying to live good lives in seas of rubbish are witness and victim to anthropogenic disasters. 'We weave through the jellyfish, bounce across their tops and plunge with surprise when we discover that some aren't jellyfish at all, but clingy, suffocating imposters.' From ancient Babylonian and Syrian stories to Disney, merfolk have lured sailors to their deaths and signalled danger; they have sung, seduced and sold themselves up to be part of the human world. Mansell holds true to these aquatic-literary inheritances, but she pushes the form further. Her merfolk are exhausted protectors of trashed ecologies – angry, vengeful and sad custodians of dying reefs and suffocating lakes. They lure humans – known in the stories as 'netters' and 'pers' (short for person) – towards danger *because* of the deadly presence of netters and their 'toxic curiosity'. If the merfolk of these stories appear more monsters than sirens, it is because of their monstrous entanglements with netters. It is because of netters' insistence on devouring all that they can see.

Two urgent questions come up as I read this work:

How is anyone to craft stories for a damaged planet?

What can stories *do* in the face of climate change, of the Anthropocene?

Mansell has brought the familiar tropes of mer fables into the realm of contemporary ecological fiction and together they amplify current threats of environmental disruption. This crafting technique might be described as sympoiesis, a weaving, a 'making' (*poiesis*) 'with' (*sym*) multiple and varied literary genres and forms. In writing about sympoiesis, Donna Haraway notes that nothing makes itself. Rather, everyone and everything is enrolled in dynamic contexts of multispecies arrangements made up of cells, organisms and ecological assemblages. These arrangements are affected by the stories we tell each other and ourselves. In the same vein, they are affected by the points of view that are and are not imagined or voiced.

One of the most significant moves Mansell makes in this collection is to attune the narrative perspective to the merfolk point of view. These stories of environmental destruction have been written from below the surface of the water, a radically alternative way to narrate the presence of humans in aquatic environments. This shift in perspective is a form of literary resistance to the status quo of environmental denigration because writing from below is a strategy that invests in alternative knowledges. Merfolk recall and account for the layers of pollution that fall out of per sight and per mind. In 'The Lake,' an isolated mer, Odel, collects fishing and camping debris that has fallen to the bottom of the lake: 'There are plastics of all colours, some thick and sturdy, others thin and suffocating; there is glass, broken and sharp, sometimes useful for removing dead scales.' As a subversive citation of Disney's *The Little Mermaid*, Odel refers to mer collection of trash as 'a treasure trove'. Mer watches as a netter casts a line, hoping for a fresh catch. But we learn that there are no fish left in the lake. Odel is hungry, too. Mer steals the worm from the freshly cast fishing line and eats it, but it does not sate. In loneliness, grief and rage, Odel imagines hooking the netter to the end of the line, of 'dragging per into the lake to watch per struggle'.

In the collection's first story, 'The Reef', the merfolk breathe with the current of their coral kingdom. They also bake and bleach along with their reef due to oceanic warming and acidification. 'If you look closely, you can see the tip of our tails turning white.' Corals' sensitivity to warming arrives as a result of their evolutionary investment in symbiosis with dinoflagellate algae, *Symbiodinium*. Warming and acidification of oceans affects this connection and reduces the fitness of coral. As fictitious coral reef symbionts, the merfolk play out the vulnerabilities of these real, lively connections. They remind readers that the fate of one species can change a whole ecosystem. Story after story, this point is driven home to us, Mansell's readers. Who will exit this text without holding this fact in mind for a time?

Many netters suffer from a condition known as shifting baseline syndrome, in which we gradually accept environmental degradation as normal when we cannot recall landscapes as they were before being reshaped. But merfolk *do* remember the layered realities of environmental shift and ruin. Again, I think of Odel who recalls how 'The river from the lake had once been bountiful, the moon's pull on the current so strong mer could ride it all the way to the ocean. Mer remembers the day the water stopped: when the world went still.' And in the final story of the collection, 'The Aquarium', the mer-narrator sings of mer home and history with a vast sad blueness, 'I sing of the eroding coasts, the paling reefs, the melting icecaps.' Mer sings to her co-captives, the dolphins, who in turn sing their own stories of trauma, displacement and degradation.

The stories collected in *Mer* call out to other works of fiction that are borne of intense climactic events. Works like Mary Shelley's *Frankenstein*, a horror story set in often stormy weather. In 1815, the year before Shelley wrote *Frankenstein*, Mount Tambora erupted in Indonesia and sent ash travelling into the stratosphere. In response, global temperatures plummeted and there was little warmth or sunlight for three years. This collection was written, in part, during Australia's most intense fire season on record. And it is to be published at a time when the Laptev Sea is yet to start its annual freeze, a delay due to exceptionally warm temperatures in northern Russia's summer, and by the intrusion of Atlantic currents into Arctic waters.

In a collection of essays called *Arts of Living on a Damaged Planet*, readers are invited into the idea that if certain species, such as jellyfish, have become monstrous, it is because of their entanglements with toxic pollution, warming waters and overfishing. The editors of the collection point out that monsters have two meanings: on the one hand 'they help us pay attention to ancient chimeric entanglements; on the other, they point us toward the monstrosities of modern Man.' The presence of merfolk in literature can do the same kind of signalling work, but I had not thought it was possible until I read the stories that have been assembled here.

At a time of intensifying climate crisis, *Mer* comes as a unique contribution to the terrain of contemporary ecological fictions, to writing environmental degradation. I want to know where Mansell's writing will go from here.

Hayley Singer

Hayley Singer's research and writing practice move across the fields of creative writing, ecofeminism and feminist animal studies. Her essays have appeared in *The Monthly*, *Art + Australia*, the *Animal Studies Journal* and she has been the ecologies columnist for the quarterly attack journal *The Lifted Brow*. Her first book, *The Fleischgeist: A haunting*, is forthcoming via The Animal Publics Series of Sydney University Press. She teaches in the Creative Writing program and the Office of Environmental Programs at the University of Melbourne.

WORKS CITED

Haraway, Donna. *Staying with the Trouble: Making Kin in the Chthulucene*. London and Durham: Duke University Press, 2016.

Tsing, A., Swanson, H., Gan, E., Bubandt, N. (eds). *Arts of Living on a Damaged Planet*. Minneapolis: University of Minnesota Press, 2017.

Acknowledgements

For all that writing is a solitary art, there sure are a lot of people to thank.

Thank you to my mum and sister for being early readers of (truly) awful novels I wrote growing up, encouraging me to pursue writing as a career.

Thank you to all those working at GSP for giving me this opportunity and working so diligently on making these stories the best they could possibly be.

Thank you to Alan Wearne, Shady Cosgrove, Mr Hume and Mr Lang and all the other teachers who shaped my writing.

Thank you to Elizabeth Weiss and Kelly Fagan for your professional insight and advice.

Finally, thank you to my partner Ji and my friends Lucy, Sunni, Lauren, Suzie and Steph for being my soundboards and supporters as I worked on this project and others. I truly couldn't have done this without your encouragement.

STAFF ACKNOWLEDGEMENTS

Mer is a highly unusual collection that deserves to be recognised for its literary innovativeness in confronting the destructive impact on our oceans of thoughtless, or deliberatively exploitative, human behaviours. The author, Samantha Amy Mansell, has been working on the stories in *Mer* for more than two years while holding down a busy job in trade publishing, and we can only praise her combination of creativity, perseverance and professionalism in bringing these stories to completion.

Publishing under COVID-19 pandemic regulations meant that the students in Grattan Street Press worked entirely remotely this semester, without physically meeting staff or student colleagues at any point in the publishing cycle. Nevertheless, the editorial team rose to the task with distinction. Copyeditors Charlotte

Armstrong, Nicole Jones and Olivia Menzies embraced the exciting challenge posed by the author's experimental vision, while production editors Michael Skinner and Sophie Wallace calmly and resourcefully set about creating the elegant object you now hold in your hands. In conditions where many bookshops were not accepting books for sale by consignment because of COVID-19, sales manager Gail Holmes enlisted everyone in the press to help place the book through their personal bookshop contacts. Thank you to the marketing team, Daisy Lucas, Banpreet Shahi and Kiran Bhat, who went all out on Bookstagram to promote *Mer*, and also to find literary bloggers to review it. Thanks too to the website team, Ian Dudley and Chloe Agius, and commissioning editor Sarah Pemberton, who all helped with sales, publicity and promotion.

Throughout the production process, students were supported by managing editor Katherine Day, digital publisher Alex Dane and design guru Mark Davis. Grattan Street Press also thanks Susannah Bowen, Hayley Singer, Aaron Mannion and Katia Ariel for their involvement and expertise. GSP's publishing would not be possible without continuing support from the School of Culture and Communication at the University of

Melbourne: thanks especially to Peter Otto, our Head of School. Finally, thanks to our printer and distributor, IngramSpark, for their speedy, professional service, especially under COVID-19 conditions.

Sybil Nolan
Publisher at Grattan Street Press

GRATTAN STREET PRESS PERSONNEL

Semester 2, 2020

Editing and Proofreading
Charlotte Armstrong – Lead Copyeditor
Olivia Kate Menzies – Copyeditor and Proofreader
Nicole Jones – Chief Proofreader and Copyeditor

Design and Production
Michael Skinner – Production Editor
Sophie Wallace – Production Editor

Sales and Marketing
Gail Holmes – Sales Manager
Daisy Lucas – Marketing Manager

Social Media
Banpreet Shahi – Social Media Officer

Submissions Officers
Kiran Bhat – Commissioning Editor
Sarah Pemberton – Commissioning Editor

Website and Blogs
Chloe Agius – MZ Editor
Ian Dudley – Website Editor and Producer

Academic Staff
Sybil Nolan
Katherine Day
Mark Davis
Alexandra Dane

ABOUT GRATTAN STREET PRESS

Grattan Street Press is a trade publisher based in Melbourne. A start-up press, we aim to publish a range of work, including contemporary literature and trade non-fiction, and to republish culturally valuable works that are out of print. The press is an initiative of the Publishing and Communications program in the School of Culture and Communication at the University of Melbourne, and is staffed by graduate students, who receive hands-on experience of every aspect of the publication process.

The press is a not-for-profit organisation that seeks to build long-term relationships with the Australian literary and publishing community. We also partner with community organisations in Melbourne and beyond to co-publish books that contribute to public knowledge and discussion.

Organisations interested in partnering with us can contact us at coordinator@grattanstreetpress.

com. Writers interested in submitting a manuscript to Grattan Street Press can contact us at editorial@ grattanstreetpress.com.

Also in the Grattan Street Shorts Series:

Something to Be Tiptoed Around
by Emma Marie Jones

In this stunning experimental mix of memoir and fictocriticism, Emma Marie Jones artfully unravels the complexities of grief, loss, memory and feminity. Drawing on elements of Greek mythology and literary theory in ways that are surprising and imaginative, Jones has created a work that is both deeply affecting and utterly human.

Available from grattanstreetpress.com and other online stores.

www.ingramcontent.com/pod-product-compliance
Ingram Content Group Australia Pty Ltd
76 Discovery Rd, Dandenong South VIC 3175, AU
AUHW010825050325
407891AU00006B/41